A GOLDEN BOOK • NEW YORK
Thomas the Tank Engine & Friends™

CREATED BY BRITT ALLCROFT

Based on The Railway Series by The Reverend W Awdry.

Thomas Breaks a Promise copyright © 2001, 2006 Gullane (Thomas) LLC. *Thomas and the Big, Big Bridge* copyright © 2001, 2003 Gullane (Thomas) LLC. *May the Best Engine Win!* copyright © 2006, 2008 Gullane (Thomas) LLC. Thomas the Tank Engine & Friends and Thomas & Friends are trademarks of Gullane (Thomas) Limited. Thomas the Tank Engine & Friends & Design is Reg. U.S. Pat. & Tm. Off. HIT and the HIT Entertainment logo are trademarks of HIT Entertainment Limited. All rights reserved. Published in the United States by Golden Books, an imprint of Random House Children's Books, a division of Random House, Inc., 1745 Broadway, New York, NY 10019, and in Canada by Random House of Canada Limited, Toronto. *Thomas Breaks a Promise* was originally published in 2001 in slightly different form as *Thomas Tells a Lie* by Random House, Inc., and in 2006 in slightly different form as *Thomas Breaks a Promise*. *Thomas and the Big, Big Bridge* was originally published in 2001 and in 2003 in slightly different form by Random House, Inc. *May the Best Engine Win!* was originally published in 2006 and in 2008 in slightly different form by Random House, Inc. Golden Books, A Golden Book, A Little Golden Book, the G colophon, and the distinctive gold spine are registered trademarks of Random House, Inc.

www.randomhouse.com/kids
www.thomasandfriends.com

Educators and librarians, for a variety of teaching tools, visit us at www.randomhouse.com/teachers
Library of Congress Control Number: 2008937621

ISBN: 978-0-375-85554-2
MANUFACTURED IN SINGAPORE
10 9 8 7 6 5 4 3 2 1
First Little Golden Book Edition 2009

Random House Children's Books supports the First Amendment and celebrates the right to read.

Thomas
Breaks a Promise

The seasons were changing on the Island of Sodor. The leaves had begun to change color, and the air was growing crisp. Thomas the Tank Engine was feeling restless.

"Summer is almost over, and I haven't had any real fun," he complained.

"You're a fussy little engine," replied Gordon. "We're not here to have fun. We're here to work."

Well, that didn't make Thomas feel any better.

"I'd rather be fussy and fun than bossy and boring!" he retorted.

The next morning, Sir Topham Hatt called the engines together.

"We're opening a new branch line tomorrow," he told them. "I need one of you to check the signals on the new line to see that they're all working properly. Who will volunteer?"

"I will," Thomas piped up. "I promise to check very carefully." Checking signals wasn't much fun, but it was better than being bossed around in the train yard.

"Off you go, then," said Sir Topham Hatt. "And be sure to check every signal, Thomas. Safety is our first concern."

Something about shiny new tracks always put
Thomas in a good mood. He whistled merrily as he rolled
along the new branch line. "Checking signals is really
useful," he thought. "Safety is our first concern."

Each time he saw a signal, Thomas made sure that the arm was in the right position. He also checked to see that the signal lamp was working, so it could be seen at night.

If the signal arm was down and the lamp was red,
that meant danger on the tracks ahead.
There were hidden junctions . . .

. . . hanging rocks . . .

. . . dangerous curves . . .

. . . and steep hills.

Thomas had almost reached the end of the new branch line when he saw the sign for a carnival. There was nothing Thomas loved more than a carnival. Oh, how he would love to go!

"If I hurry to the carnival now, I can check the rest of the signals later," he told himself. And with that, Thomas turned off and headed into the countryside.

Carnival
TODAY ONLY!

The carnival was splendid. There were games and rides and cotton candy. And there were lots of children.

"Look, it's Thomas!" they cried, and ran to greet their favorite blue engine.

When Thomas got back to the train yard, Sir Topham Hatt was waiting.

"You've been gone a long time, Thomas," he said. "You must have done a very thorough job of checking the signals on the new branch line."

"Yes, sir," peeped Thomas. But suddenly he realized that he'd forgotten to go back and finish the job. He had broken his promise! But how could he tell that to Sir Topham Hatt?

"Good." Sir Topham Hatt beamed. "Then everything is ready for tomorrow's grand opening."

Thomas gulped. What if there was trouble? What if one of the unchecked signals didn't work?

"I know," thought Thomas. "I'll get up very early tomorrow and go out to check the rest of the signals before the grand opening."

That night, Percy was being loaded for his mail run when a call came into the station. Rain had washed out a section of track on the mail route. Percy would have to find a way around.

"Don't worry, Percy." Sir Topham Hatt smiled. "You can take the new branch line."

Off Percy went, pulling two big cars loaded with mail.

The rain fell heavily. Each time Percy saw a red signal lamp, he slowed carefully until he had passed the dangerous spot. Then suddenly, in the dark, Percy passed another signal. The lamp was not lit, so he didn't see it until too late. The arm was down, for danger! Percy slammed on his brakes, but the rain made the tracks slippery. And there it was ahead—a *very* dangerous curve.

"Oh, no!" cried Percy. He closed his eyes and did his best to hold on through the turn.

CRASH! One of the mail cars flew off the tracks and was smashed to bits. Percy shivered with fear from his close call.

The next morning, Thomas awoke and sneaked out of his shed. Then he saw Percy returning with Sir Topham Hatt.

"Percy has had a terrible fright," Sir Topham said sternly. "He almost derailed because of a signal lamp that didn't work. How could such a thing have happened, Thomas?"

"Oh, sir! I'm so sorry, sir," Thomas sputtered. And it all came rushing out—about the carnival, and the children, and about how he'd forgotten to go back and finish the job.

"I'm sorry I broke my promise, sir," said Thomas sheepishly. "I just wanted to be part of the fun, and then I forgot."

"There will be no fun for you for quite some time," Sir Topham Hatt scolded. "Percy will run your branch line until you've gone and checked every signal on my railway—twice!"

And now, every time Thomas passes a signal, he
checks it twice, just to be safe.

Gordon likes to tease him. "Fussy little Thomas
certainly is fussy about signals."

"Peep, peep!" says Thomas. "Safety is our first
concern."

It was a special day for the railway!

"We are here to launch the new rail line through the Mountains of Sodor," Sir Topham Hatt announced. "Today we open the big, big bridge!"

What wonderful news! Everyone cheered. The mountains
were beautiful. The people of Sodor couldn't wait to visit them.

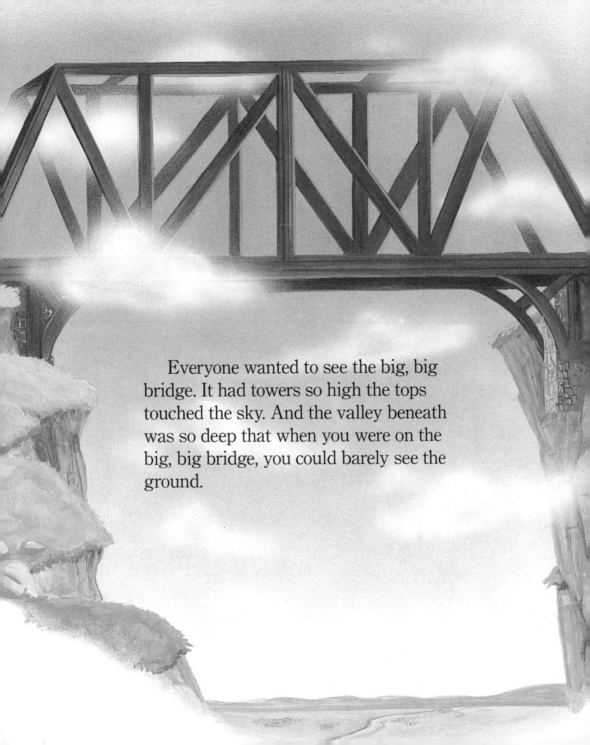

Everyone wanted to see the big, big bridge. It had towers so high the tops touched the sky. And the valley beneath was so deep that when you were on the big, big bridge, you could barely see the ground.

Thomas was excited about the new rail line.
"This really is a special day!" he said happily.
Then Henry chugged up to Thomas. The big engine frowned.

"I don't want to go to the mountains," Henry said nervously.
"It's windy up there—very, very windy." Henry didn't like the wind.
Henry didn't like rain or snow or hail, either.

"You're a big engine, Henry!" Thomas said. "You shouldn't be
afraid of a little wind."

But Henry was afraid. And that made Thomas a bit afraid, too.

"Gordon! Henry! Thomas! Hitch up your coaches!" called Sir Topham Hatt. "It's time for your first trip to the mountains."

Percy and James were glad they didn't have to go to the mountains. They were afraid to cross the big, big bridge, too.

"There's nothing to be afraid of," Thomas insisted, in a voice loud enough for Percy and James to hear. "It will be easy to cross the big, big bridge."

Thomas and Henry chugged to the platform. Gordon the Express Engine was already there. His coaches were full of passengers.

Annie and Clarabel were soon hitched behind Thomas. "Hurry, hurry," they called.

"All aboard!" cried the conductor.

Sir Topham Hatt turned to the crowd and waved his hat one last time.

Toot, toot, Gordon whistled. "Follow me!"

In a burst of steam, the big blue engine was off.

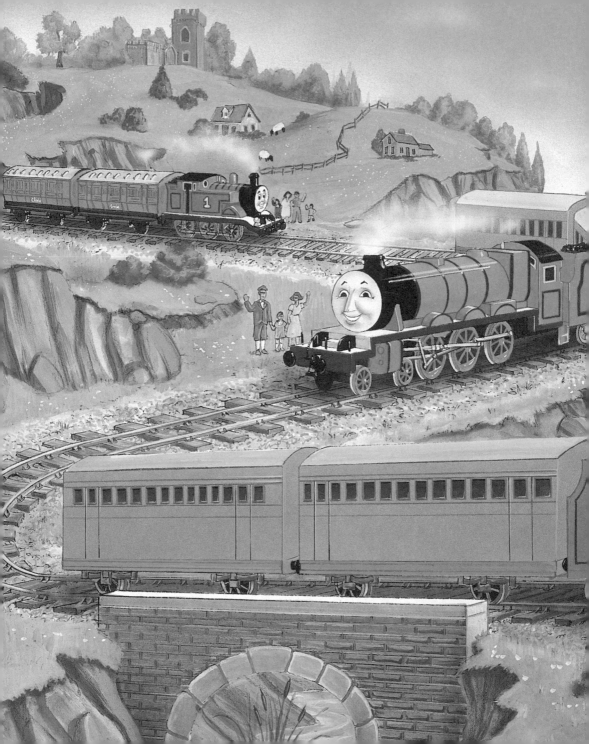

Soon the trains were rolling through the countryside in a long line. Gordon took the lead. Behind him chugged Henry. Then, because he was the smallest, came Thomas.

All along the way, people came out of their houses and cheered when they saw the trains go by.

At the foot of the mountain, Henry slowed to a crawl. "These mountains are much too high," he moaned. "I *can't* go. I'm afraid of heights!"

"Don't be silly," said Thomas bravely. "I'll be right here behind you."

But Henry didn't budge. He was very nervous. And that made Thomas nervous, too.

"Come on!" Thomas gently pushed Henry. "We have to go!"

The brand-new tracks were smooth and shiny, but Henry barely moved along them. The truth was, Henry didn't want to reach the top of the mountain, because then he'd have to cross the big, big bridge.

"If Percy and James and Henry are all afraid," thought Thomas, "maybe *I* should be frightened, too!"

The tracks grew steep as Thomas and Henry puffed up the mountain. They could hardly keep up with Gordon. The big blue engine rushed ahead.

Gordon was a strong engine. The steep tracks didn't tire him at all!

"Wait for us!" Henry called. But Gordon climbed higher and higher, until he was out of sight.

"I don't think I can make it," Henry groaned, his steam giving out at last. "This mountain is too steep!"

"Keep going!" Thomas urged him. "We can't let a little mountain stop us."

But Thomas was having trouble chugging up the steep mountain, too. And he was beginning to worry about crossing the big, big bridge.

Finally, Thomas and Henry arrived at the top of the mountain.

There it was—the big, big bridge! And it was high. It was windy up there, too—*very* windy.

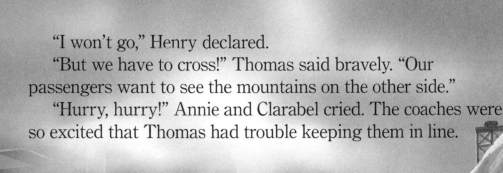

"I won't go," Henry declared.

"But we have to cross!" Thomas said bravely. "Our passengers want to see the mountains on the other side."

"Hurry, hurry!" Annie and Clarabel cried. The coaches were so excited that Thomas had trouble keeping them in line.

Thomas searched the tracks ahead. Gordon was nowhere to be seen. He had already crossed the bridge and rolled into the mountains beyond.

Thomas and Henry were alone.

"I'll go first," Thomas said at last. "Then you can follow me, Henry."

"If the wind blows, close your eyes," Henry said. "That way you won't see anything scary."

Click-clack! Click-clack! Click-clack! Thomas began
to cross the bridge.

Thomas looked up. He could see cottony clouds
touching the top of the bridge.

Nervously, he looked down. But the bridge was so
high he couldn't see the ground.

A sudden gust of wind shook the bridge. This scared Thomas, and he closed his eyes so tightly that he couldn't see where he was going.

Click-clack! Click-clack! Click-CRASH! Thomas came to a sudden stop. He opened one eye for a quick peek. "Oh, no!" he cried. His wheels were off the track!

"Are you all right, Thomas?" called Henry.

"I'm stuck," Thomas said glumly. "I couldn't see where I was going and my front wheels have jumped the track."

Just then, Gordon returned. He frowned when he saw Thomas stuck in the middle of the bridge.

"Go find Harold," Gordon called to Henry. Relieved, Henry
backed down the mountain to find the helicopter.

Thomas kept his eyes closed. He was too afraid to look. But
inside his coaches, the passengers enjoyed the wonderful view.

Finally, Thomas heard the whirl of rotors. Harold was
here to rescue him!

Slowly, Thomas opened his eyes. He looked at the blue
sky above and the green mountains all around.

"What a lovely view!" he exclaimed. "I was silly to shut
my eyes. I almost missed everything."

"Hitch the rope to your buffer and hold on!" Harold cried.

In no time at all, Harold had lifted Thomas back onto the tracks. Thomas backed up to where Henry waited.

"Come on, Henry," said Thomas. "The view is spectacular. I should never have been afraid."

With that, Thomas turned and chugged happily across the big, big bridge. Henry watched in wonder.

"If he's not afraid, maybe I shouldn't be, either!" Henry decided.

Slowly, the big green engine made his way across the bridge, too.

Soon Thomas and Henry arrived at the station house.
The mountains were really lovely. Everyone was happy to
have seen them. But Thomas was the happiest one of all.
He was proud that he had crossed the big, big bridge!

Early one morning on the Island of Sodor, Sir Topham Hatt came to the Yard. Thomas and Emily were preparing for a busy day.

Thomas always worked very hard. He was proud to be a Really Useful Engine.

Emily was new. She wanted to prove that she was Really Useful, too. She hoped that Sir Topham Hatt would see how excited she was to start the day.

"Thomas, there's a lot to do today. I hope that everything gets done on time," said Sir Topham Hatt.

"Why should Thomas get all the work?" asked Emily. "I can do anything he can. I'm faster than him, too!"

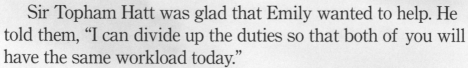

Sir Topham Hatt was glad that Emily wanted to help. He told them, "I can divide up the duties so that both of you will have the same workload today."

Emily knew it would be a long day, but she smiled. She told Thomas, "Now you'll see what I can do."

Thomas was used to long days. "Emily, this might be too much work for you," he teased. "You should let me do more."

"*Pfffft!*" she puffed. "I'll race you! Whoever finishes and makes it back to the station first is the winner."

"Let's go!" peeped Thomas.

With a *Peep!* and a *Poop!,* Thomas and Emily left
the station side by side.

Emily's first stop was the Quarry. She'd brought crates full of new tools, and she had to stay in place while the workers unloaded them. After all the crates were taken away, the workers hitched her to freight cars full of large stones.

Emily knew that Really Useful Engines were supposed to be good at waiting. But it was difficult for her to be patient.

"Please hurry," she told the workers. "I don't want Thomas to get ahead!"

While Emily was at the Quarry, Thomas was running his Branch Line.

He moved from station to station. At every stop, more passengers got off and Annie and Clarabel got lighter and lighter.

"I'll bet I'm pulling ahead of Emily already," thought Thomas.

Along the way to his last station, Thomas saw
Emily. She was going to Suddery with stone from
the Quarry.

"There you are, slowcoach!" she called.

Thomas laughed. "That stone looks awfully heavy!" he said.

He hoped that Emily would get tired from hauling such a heavy load.

Thomas' second job was to deliver a load of barrels to the docks. He had to wait for the barrels to be moved onto boats.

Thomas was not a very patient engine, but he knew it would do no good to win the race if he didn't do his job just right.

"The other engines will tease me forever if Emily wins," he thought. He would have to go extra fast to his next stop.

"Is it time to go back to the Shed?" he asked his Driver.

"You still have to haul some Troublesome Trucks to Cronk," said the Driver.

Troublesome Trucks were always
bumping and bashing. Thomas had
to work hard to keep them in line.
"Don't try anything funny!"
he said as they left the station.

But soon Thomas had to stop at a signal.

The Signalman explained, "Some rocks have fallen onto the tracks. You'll have to wait until the way is clear."

"Oh, bother," said Thomas. "I wonder where Emily is now."

Emily had left Suddery. Her final job was a Special along the mountain route.

On the way, she passed Thomas, who was stopped at the signal.

"Poor Thomas!" she called to him. "Looks like you're stuck!"

Emily sped up.

She saw a sign warning of a winding track ahead, but she didn't want to slow down and risk losing the race.

The track was difficult, and she was going too fast. Her Driver told her to slow down.

But it was too late. As Emily took a turn, one of her trucks tipped over!

Now she had to wait for help. "Thomas will get ahead for sure," she thought.

Thomas was having better luck. The rocks had been cleared, and he was almost done with his last job of the day.

He saw Harvey moving on the opposite track. "Hello, Harvey," he peeped. "Where are you headed?"

"Emily's hit a spot of trouble up the line," said Harvey. "Nothing to worry about."

Emily was glad to see Harvey. She thanked him for his help.

"I'll take the rest of the path slowly," she said. "If I'm more careful, I still might beat Thomas."

Thomas was having some difficulty with the Troublesome
Trucks. They made him go faster than he wanted to. But his brakes
were strong and he was able to stay on the track.

Once the Troublesome Trucks were unhitched, he sped away
toward home. "I hope Emily isn't there yet," he thought.

The sun was nearly setting by the time Thomas arrived at
the Yard.

He didn't see Emily anywhere.

Emily arrived only a minute later. When she saw
Thomas, she frowned. She had really wanted to beat him.

Thomas saw her sad expression. He knew that *he* would
have been sad if he had lost, so he decided not to brag.

"That was a close race," he said.

"You won fair and square," said Emily.

"But I'll beat you tomorrow," she added.
Thomas laughed. "We'll see about that!"